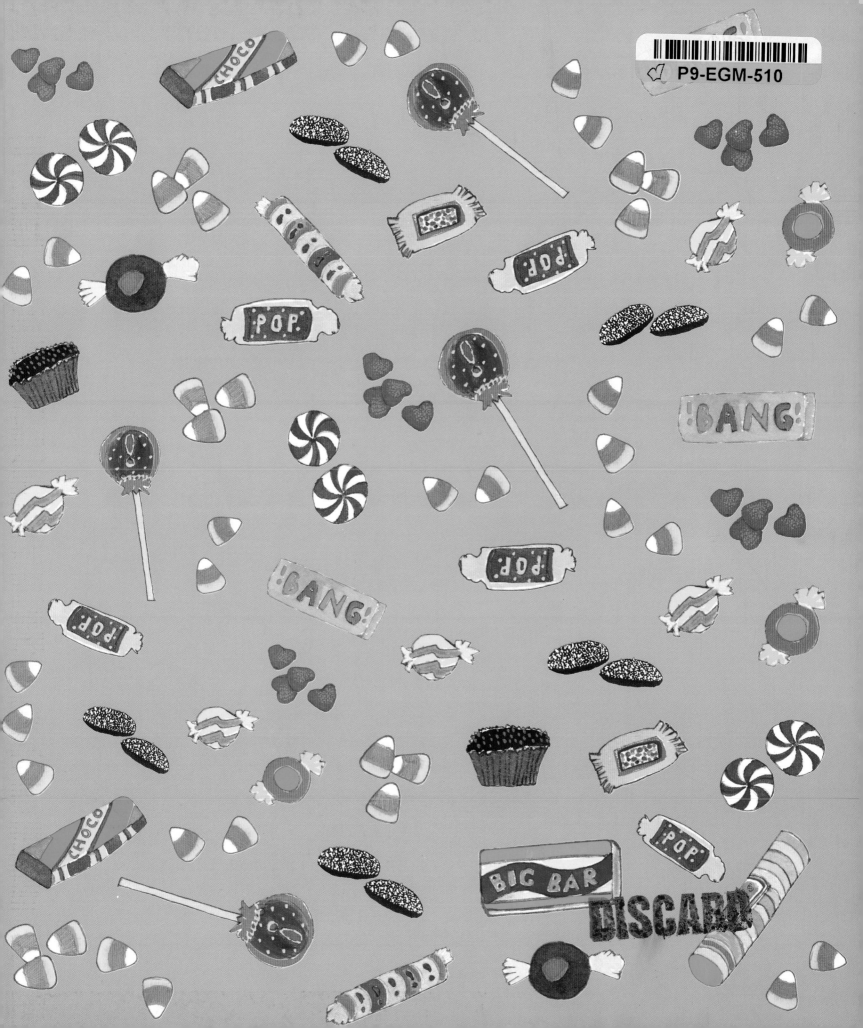

CHICAGO PUBLIC LIBRARY

for me
for you
for later

FIRST STEPS TO SPENDING, SHARING, AND SAVING™

City of Chicago
Mayor Rahm Emanuel

Chicago
Public
Library

chicagopubliclibrary.org

Chicago
Public
Library Foundation

PNC Grow Up Great™

MAX'S Bunny Business

LEMONADE
10¢ A CUP

ROSEMARY WELLS

VIKING

VIKING
Published by Penguin Group
Penguin Young Readers Group, 345 Hudson Street, New York, New York 10014, U.S.A.
Penguin Group (Canada), 90 Eglinton Avenue East, Suite 700, Toronto, Ontario,
Canada M4P 2Y3 (a division of Pearson Penguin Canada Inc.)

Penguin Books Ltd, Registered Offices: 80 Strand, London WC2R 0RL, England

First published in 2008 by Viking, a division of Penguin Young Readers Group

5   7   9   10   8   6   4

LIBRARY OF CONGRESS CATALOGING-IN-PUBLICATION DATA
Wells, Rosemary.
Max's bunny business / Rosemary Wells.
p. cm.
Summary: Ruby and her friend Louise set up a lemonade stand to earn money
to buy matching rings, but Max foils their plan.
ISBN 978-0-670-01105-6 (hardcover)
[1. Moneymaking projects–Fiction. 2. Brothers and sisters–Fiction.
3. Rabbits–Fiction.] I. Title.
PZ7.W46843Masfh 2008
[E]–dc22
2007040461

Manufactured in China
Set in Minister

The telephone rang.

"I'll get it!" said Max's sister, Ruby.

It was Louise.

"I'm wearing the Fire Angel shimmering necklace!" said Louise.

"I'm wearing the Fire Angel twinkling bracelet!" said Ruby.

"I saw two Fire Angel flashing rings in the store!" said Louise.

"We need to make two dollars to buy them!" said Ruby.

Louise brought over the lemons.

Ruby got out the card table and the umbrella.

"We can sell lemonade at ten cents a cup!" said Ruby.

"We will need to sell twenty cups," said Louise.

Louise and Ruby made a big sign.
Max wanted to make a sign, too.
"You can't write, Max," said Ruby.

Max wanted to squeeze the lemons.
"I'll do it, Max," said Louise.

Max wanted to pour the lemonade
into the cups. But he poured it onto
the sidewalk by mistake.

"Max," said Ruby, "we are running a business! You go play in your fire engine!"

But Max did not want to play in his fire engine.
Instead, he ran up the stairs . . .

and into the closet. On the top shelf was a
big bag of long-forgotten Halloween candy.

Max put the candy on the sidewalk outside the house.

Max made a big sign that said, "Candy for sale!"

And he opened for business.

Down the street, Ruby and Louise had so many customers they couldn't see straight.
"We've sold ten cups!" said Louise.

"That's one dollar," said Ruby. "Halfway there!"
Grandma waited in line for a cup of lemonade.
"This line is too long!" said Grandma.

So Grandma went over to Max.

Max sold her all his candy for one dollar.

They decided to go to Pinkie's Novelty Store
and spend Max's dollar.

Ruby and Louise were cleaned out.

They'd sold twenty cups of lemonade.

"Enough for two rings!" said Louise.

Ruby and Louise rode their bikes as fast as they could, but they were too late to buy the last Fire Angel flashing ring in Pinkie's store.

Grandma and Max made lemonade
for everyone.
"Where have you girls been?"
asked Grandma.

"We had to buy on-again off-again sparkling earrings!" said Ruby.
"Someone else bought the last flashing ring!" said Louise.

"I wonder who?" said Grandma.

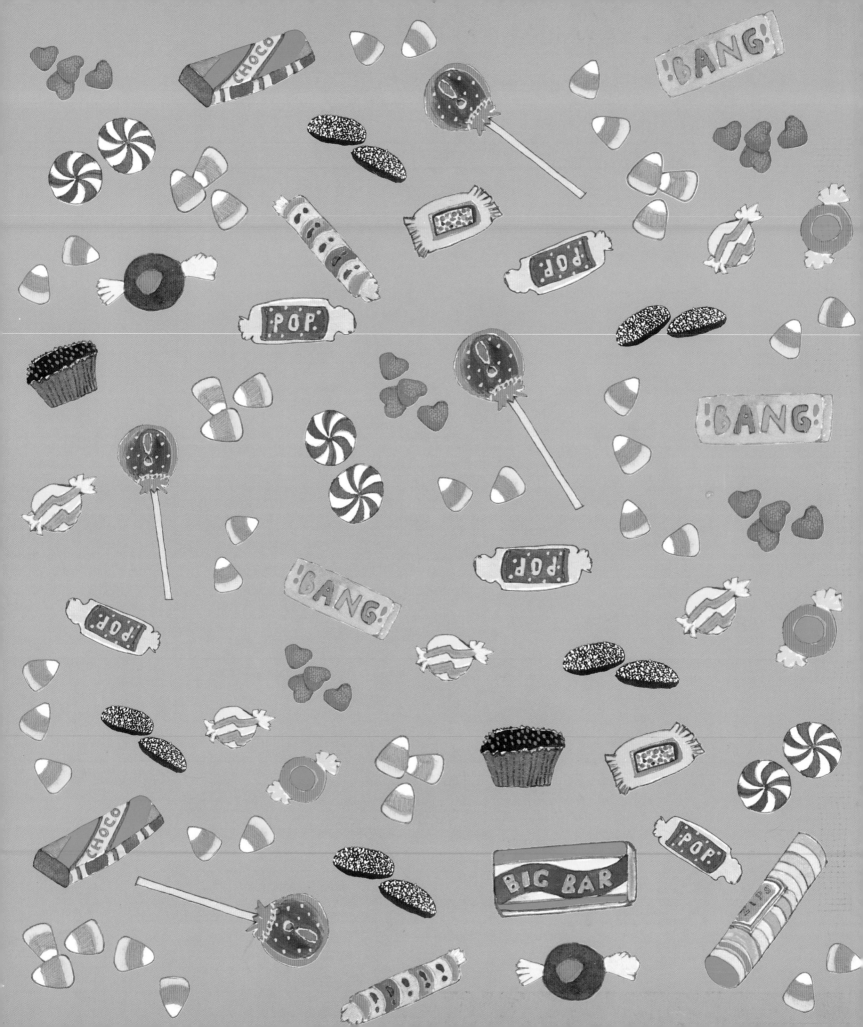